W9-AQB-686

W9-AQB-686

13502461

Clarion Books
a Houghton Mifflin Company imprint
215 Park Avenue South, New York, NY 10003
Text copyright © 1994 by Linda DaVolls.
Illustrations copyright © 1994 by Andy DaVolls.

Published in the United States 1994 by arrangement with Reed
Consumer Books Limited, Michelin House, 81 Fulham Road, London SW3 6RB, England.

All rights reserved.

For information about permission to reproduce selections from
this book, write to Permissions, Houghton Mifflin Company,
215 Park Avenue South, New York, NY 10003

Printed in China

Library of Congress Cataloging-in-Publication Data

DaVolls, Linda.
Tano & Binti: two chimpanzees return to the wild/ by Linda DaVolls;
illustrated by Andy DaVolls.
p.   cm.
Summary: Describes the experiences of two young chimpanzees that
were raised in the London Zoo and then released in Gambia, where an
older chimpanzee helped them learn to survive in the wild.
ISBN 0-395-68701-2
1. Wildlife reintroduction—Gambia—Juvenile literature.
2. Chimpanzee—Gambia—Juvenile literature. [1. Chimpanzees.
2. Wildlife reintroduction. 3. Wildlife conservation.]
I. DaVolls, Andy, ill. II. Title. III. Title: Tano and Binti.
QL84.6.G25D38 1994
599.88'44—dc20   93—25403
                                                         CIP
                                                         AC

10   9   8   7   6   5   4   3   2   1

TANO & BINTI

Two Chimpanzees Return to the Wild

Andy and Linda DaVolls

CLARION BOOKS · NEW YORK

WITHDRAWN

Jefferson-Madison
Regional Library
Charlottesville, Virginia

Chimpanzees once lived in the forests throughout Central Africa. Much of the forest growth has now been destroyed, causing chimpanzee populations to decline. Chimps are no longer secure anywhere in the wild. Zoos and wild animal parks have developed programs committed to conserving endangered species that ensures the animals will survive even if the forests do not.

It is our hope that one day the forests will be restored, so that all chimpanzees will be secure in the wild.

In 1975, two chimps born at London Zoo had the chance to return to Africa.
Their reintroduction was made possible by Stella Brewer of The Gambian Chimpanzee Rehabilitation Project who, with the help of semi-wild chimps living in a protected area, taught the young chimps the ways of the forest.

The story of Tano and Binti is based on the true story of these chimps.

Tano and his younger sister Binti peered out of their crate in
bewilderment. They had just arrived after a long journey from
London Zoo in the African forest that was to be their new home.
They would need to learn many new skills to survive.

Tano crept out of the crate and touched the dry, leafy ground.
He dug curiously into the soil, letting it fall through his fingers.

Satisfied that it would not harm him, he began to scream excitedly.

There were strange, new sounds in the forest. Tano and Binti
huddled together under a small bush. The midday sun was hot
and they soon drifted off to sleep.

They were startled awake by the sound of rustling in the bushes.
They looked up to see an older chimpanzee approaching them.

This was Amber. Amber was a long-time resident
of the forest. She held out her hand in friendship
and made a soft, panting sound that meant the
young chimps shouldn't be frightened.

Tano and Binti raced to Amber and hooted in her
ear in greeting. Soon the three chimps were cuddling
together. They spent the afternoon grooming one
another, until Tano became restless: He was hungry.

Amber led the way to a fig tree and placed a fig in Tano's palm.
He sniffed the fig cautiously at first, then he slowly bit into the
sweet, ripe fruit. When he grunted enthusiastically, Binti joined
them. All three chimps feasted until they were full.

Amber decided to take a nap, but Tano and Binti were full of energy. They played a chasing, wrestling, and tickling game in the trees.

At dusk, Amber led them to a stream. She cupped her hands and plunged them into the cool, running water. Tano and Binti watched her drink and did the same.

Night fell. Tano and Binti whimpered in fright as the trees began to cast dark shadows and the forest came alive with night sounds. Amber climbed a tall tree and folded a mass of lush green leaves into a large, cozy nest. The young chimps snuggled close to Amber's side all night.

The three chimps climbed down from their nest when the forest birds began their morning song at sunrise.

Amber led the way to a tall mound in a clearing. Tano and Binti watched as Amber wiggled a long stem of grass into a hole in the mound. She pulled the stem out and ate three fat termites that were clinging to it. The young chimps were soon fishing for termites too.

As the days passed, Amber showed Tano and Binti all kinds of
edible fruit, seeds, bark, and berries. They learned which leaves
were the juiciest and which grasses the sweetest. She taught them
to use stones as hammers to break the hard shells of pods and nuts.

The chimps learned to build their own nests for sleeping at night, though Amber was always close by. The forest was no longer a strange place. The forest gave them everything they needed to live well.

But one morning, Binti woke to find Amber's nest empty.

Binti ran to her brother in distress. Amber was gone. The chimps clung tightly to each other. They were now on their own.

The two chimps remembered every lesson Amber had taught them as they traveled alone during the next few weeks. They missed Amber, but they could take care of themselves.

One day, more than a year after Tano and Binti had first arrived in the African forest, Amber came back. The two chimps shrieked with excitement when they saw her and ran to hug her. Amber hugged them back, as excited to see them as they were to see her. Suddenly Tano and Binti noticed . . .

. . . that clinging to Amber's tummy was a tiny baby! Amber gently placed the baby's fingers on Tano's arm, and he grinned. Binti panted softly into the baby's ear.

A large male approached and looked affectionately at the new baby. He took notice of Tano and Binti. It was clear that he approved of including them in their band. Tano and Binti would no longer have to depend only on each other to find the best places to eat and sleep. The forest was now truly their home.

SEP   1994

SEP   1994